>+ A FABER PICTURE BOOK +<

A
Harry
& Lil
Story

The Hog, the Shrew and the Hullabaloo

Julia Copus

Illustrated by
Eunyoung Seo

ff

FABER & FABER

It was night in the village — a still, dark night — and Harry the Hog was sleeping tight.

In her house at the foot of Piggyback Hill,
also asleep, was Candy Stripe Lil.

Now Harry the Hog was a champion sleeper:
no other hog could sleep longer or deeper.
That night, he'd finished his exercise

(two hog-jumps,

three sit-ups,

four blinks of the eyes)

and at last he was snug in his blankets again,
happily dreaming his hog-dreams when . . .

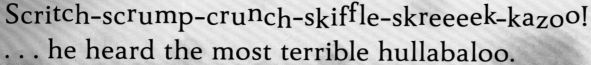
Scritch-scrump-crunch-skiffle-skreeeek-kazoo!
. . . he heard the most terrible hullabaloo.

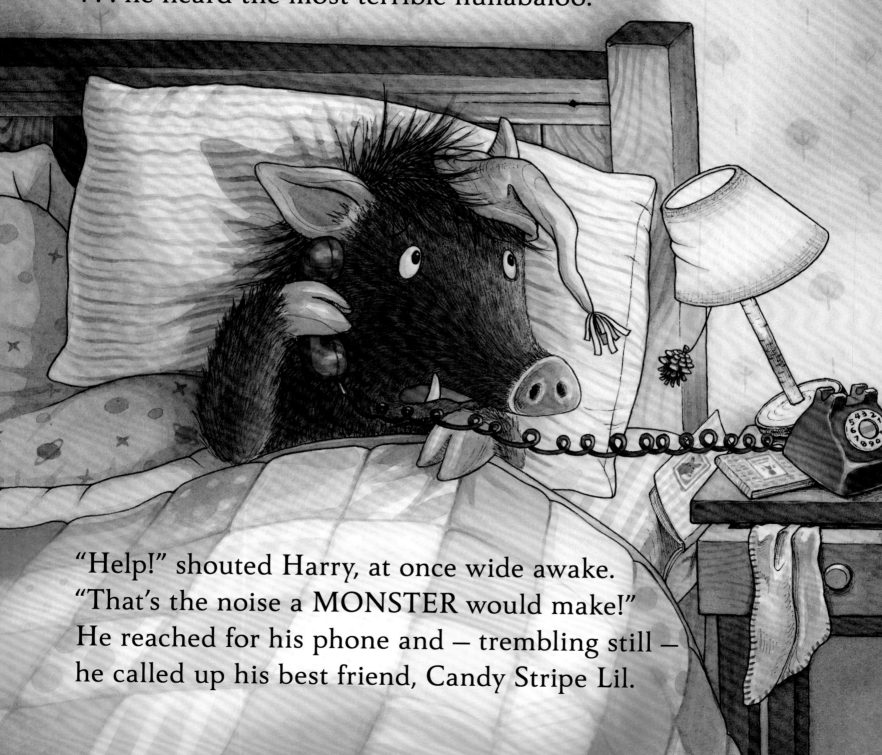

"Help!" shouted Harry, at once wide awake.
"That's the noise a MONSTER would make!"
He reached for his phone and — trembling still —
he called up his best friend, Candy Stripe Lil.

When Lil arrived, she took off her jacket:
"We'll soon find out what made such a racket.
But for now," she said, "we must try to rest."
"If I *can*," Harry said. "I'll do my best."

Then "*Shh!*" squeaked Lil. "I heard a scuffle.
What *is* that, making such a kerfuffle?"

They ran to the window . . .

lifted the latch . . .

and opened it.

There, in the cabbage patch,
in the midst of the murk they could just make out
the black and white stripes of a badger's snout.

"Hello!" called Lil.
A scuffle . . .
A crunch . .

"Hullo there!" said Badger. "I'm just having lunch.
I often feel peckish at this sort of time
for a beetle or two and a sip of slug slime."

Harry looked at Lil and shook his head.
"That wasn't the sound I heard," he said.
"That's only the sound a badger can make.
It was something much *scarier* that kept me awake."

So they crept up the staircase, bedward-bound;
the house was creaking all around.

Up they went through the not-quite-light,
through the in-between of day and night.

Then *"Shh!"* said Harry. "I heard a cry —
somewhere outside, in the moon-pale sky."

It came again: screeeech! This time, Harry fled
and burrowed snout-first under the bed.

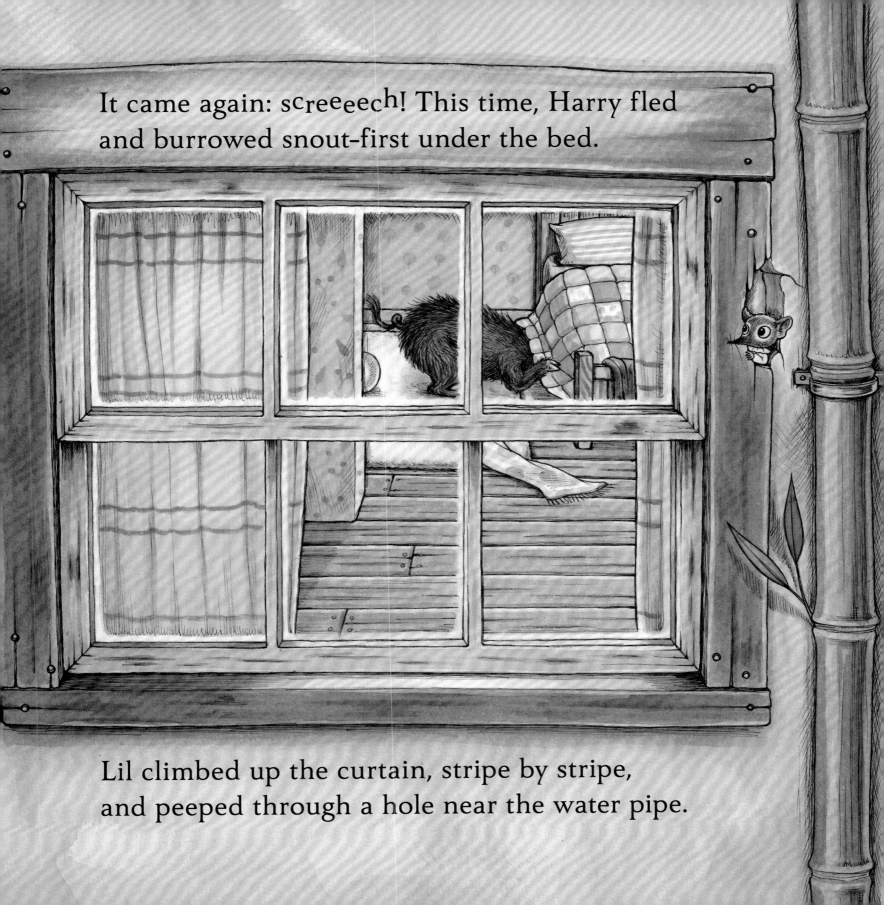

Lil climbed up the curtain, stripe by stripe,
and peeped through a hole near the water pipe.

Very close, on the branch of a silver birch,
a busy barn owl had come to perch.

"Hello there," squeaked Lil. "You gave us a fright!"
"I'm just working," said Owl. "During the night
there's so much to do." And she heaved her chest.
"I've stopped to give my wings a rest."

At once Harry wriggled
from under the bed.
"That wasn't the sound
I heard," he said.

"That's only the sound
an owl can make.
It was something much
wilder that kept me awake."

So back they went through the not-quite-light,
through the in-between of day and night.

This time, they almost made it to bed.
"Goodnight," said Lil. "Goodnight," Harry said.

Lil put on her bed-socks, pulled them tight,
and was reaching up to switch off the light
when . . .

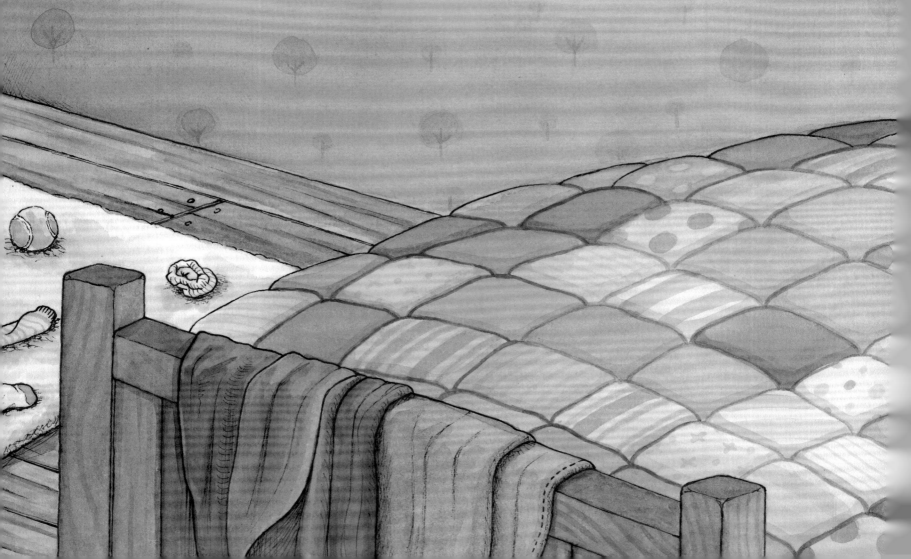

"*Shh!*" said Harry. "I heard a kraark!
Somewhere down there in the shadowy dark."

Down they rushed to the locked front door
and very gently, paw by paw,
Lil climbed onto Harry, still in her socks,
and together they peeked through the letter box.

There by the pond, on a large, flat stone,
a frog was croaking away on his own.

"Hello!" called Harry. "Kraaaark!" Frog replied.
"How I love to be out by the water's side,
on a night like this, with the stars above,
and sing serenades to my one true love."

Harry looked at Lil and shook his head.
"That wasn't the sound I heard," he said.
"That's only the sound a frog can make.
It was something much *fiercer* that kept me awake."

It was almost dawn when they made it to bed.
"It looks like the monster's gone," Lil said.

Out in the garden all was still.
Not a wisp of a whisper was heard until . . .

With a scuffle, a screech and a kraark, kraark,
the strangest sound came out of the dark.
"That's it!" Harry cried. "That's the sound I heard.
Too fierce for a frog, too wild for a bird."

"I suppose we should take a look," said Lil.
And, quickly, she climbed up onto the sill.

In the glow of the moon,
in its silvery sheen,
was the ugliest shape
you've ever seen.

"What *is* it?" gasped Lil. "What on earth can it be?"
She opened the window and leaned out to see.

Slowly, as the sun rose over the hill,
the strange-looking shape became stranger still.

They looked . . .
then stared . . .
then stood there, agog,
as the shape became . . .

Badger and Owl and Frog!

Owl was screeching,
Frog was croaking,
Badger was rootling,
scraping and poking.

"What a racket!" cried Harry. "What a parade!
Surely that can't be what made me afraid?
A silly old badger, an owl and a frog?
It takes more than that to frighten a hog!"

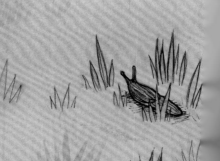

And he climbed back into
his bed, with a yawn.

"Poor Harry!" laughed Owl. "But now it's past dawn,
the three of *us* must get to bed."
"Goodbye then," said Lil. "Good *night*!" Owl said.

Owl and her friends had just snuggled under

when a noise shook the air like the rumbling of thunder.

From deep in the house, behind the closed door,
Harry the Hog had started to snore.